Highlights Puzzle Readers

LEVEL **2**

LET'S READ,
READ, READ

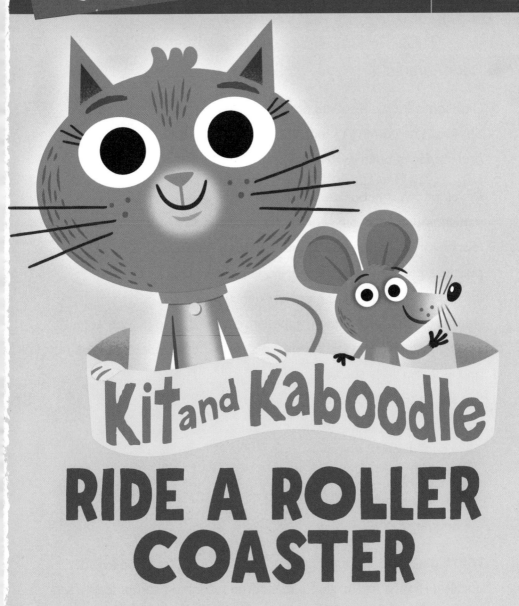

Kit and Kaboodle
RIDE A ROLLER COASTER

By Michelle Portice
Art by Mitch Mortimer

HIGHLIGHTS PRESS

Honesdale, Pennsylvania

Stories + Puzzles = Reading Success!

Dear Parents,

Highlights Puzzle Readers are an innovative approach to learning to read that combines puzzles and stories to build motivated, confident readers.

Developed in collaboration with reading experts, the stories and puzzles are seamlessly integrated so that readers are encouraged to read the story, solve the puzzles, and then read the story again. This helps increase vocabulary and reading fluency and creates a satisfying reading experience for any kind of learner. In addition, solving Hidden Pictures puzzles fosters important reading and learning skills such as:

- shape and letter recognition
- letter-sound relationships
- visual discrimination
- logic
- flexible thinking
- sequencing

With high-interest stories, humorous characters, and trademark puzzles, Highlights Puzzle Readers offer a winning combination for inspiring young learners to love reading.

This
is Kit.

This is
Kaboodle.

They love to travel.
You can help them on
each adventure.

As you read the story,
find the objects in each
Hidden Pictures
puzzle.

Then check the
Packing List on
pages 30–31 to make
sure you found everything.

Happy reading!

4

Kit and Kaboodle are going
to Wonder Park. They are ready
for an exciting day!

"Wonder Park has
the fastest roller coaster," says Kit.

"It's also the tallest roller coaster,"
says Kaboodle.

"We're here!" says Kit.

"Not yet," says Kaboodle.

Kit and Kaboodle ride a tram.

"We're here!" says Kit.

"Not yet," says Kaboodle.

They go through the gate.

"We're here!" says Kit.

"Yes, we're here!" says Kaboodle.

"Let's play a game," says Kaboodle. "That game looks fun."

"We need to buy tickets to play," says Kit.

"I packed some money we can use to buy tickets," says Kaboodle.

He looks in his bag.

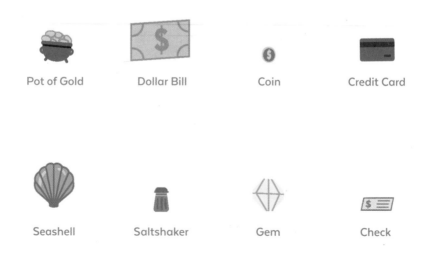

Pot of Gold   Dollar Bill   Coin   Credit Card

Seashell   Saltshaker   Gem   Check

"What a fun prize!" says Kit.

"I hope it will fit in my pack."

"What a fun prize!" says Kaboodle.

"I hope it will fit in my bag."

SLAM DUNK

"Should we ride the roller coaster next?" asks Kit.

"Not yet," says Kaboodle. "What time is the parade?"

"The parade is starting now!" says Kit.

"I packed a few things
we can use to cheer," says Kaboodle.

He looks in his bag.

Flag

Pinwheel

Glow Stick

Horn

Balloon

Pompom

Magic Wand

Foam Finger

TASTY★TREATS

DRINKS!

"What a fun parade!" says Kaboodle.

"Should we ride the roller coaster next?" asks Kit.

"I'm not sure," says Kaboodle.
"It's very fast. Let's ride that ride."

The ride goes slowly up, up, up.

Then the ride goes down very fast.

SPLASH!

"What a fun ride!" says Kaboodle.
"But now we're all wet."

"What are we going to do?" asks Kit.

"I packed a few things
we can use to dry off," says Kaboodle.

He looks in his bag.

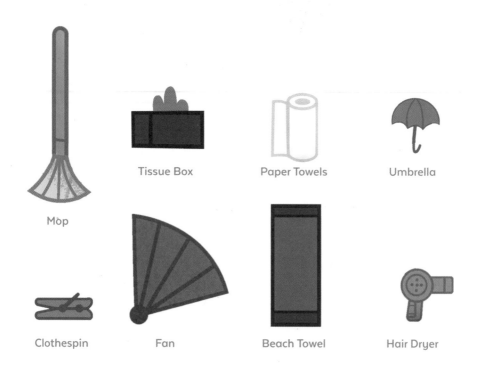

Mop

Tissue Box

Paper Towels

Umbrella

Clothespin

Fan

Beach Towel

Hair Dryer

"Should we ride the roller coaster next?" asks Kit.

"I'm not sure," says Kaboodle. "It's very tall."

"Let's ride this ride next," says Kit.

The ride goes up, up, up very high.

"Look at the view!" says Kaboodle.

The ride goes down, down, down.

"That was a fun ride!" says Kaboodle.
"But now I'm hungry."

"Let's have a snack," says Kit.

"I packed a few snacks,"
says Kaboodle.

He looks in his bag.

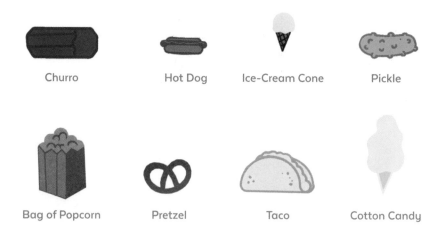

Churro

Hot Dog

Ice-Cream Cone

Pickle

Bag of Popcorn

Pretzel

Taco

Cotton Candy

Kit and Kaboodle swing on tall swings.

"*Whee!*" says Kit.

They slide down long slides.

"*Whee!*" says Kaboodle.

They bump in fast bumper cars.

"*Whee!*" says Kit.

"*Whee!*" says Kaboodle.

"Those rides were so much fun!" says Kit.
"Should we ride the roller coaster?"

"Yes!" says Kaboodle.
"I'm ready to ride the roller coaster."

"I'm ready, too," says Kit.

"I packed a few things we can do
while we wait in line," says Kaboodle.

He looks in his bag.

Jump Rope

Television

Crayon

Puzzle Piece

Book

Ball of Yarn

Playing Cards

Guitar

"It's our turn," says Kaboodle.

"Hooray!" says Kit.

The ride goes slowly up, up, up very high.

Then the ride goes down very fast.

"*Whee!*" says Kit.

"*Whee!*" says Kaboodle.

"We did it," says Kaboodle.
"We rode the roller coaster!"

"It was very tall and very fast," says Kit.

"And it was very fun!" says Kaboodle.

"We make a good team," says Kit.

"Where should we go on our next trip?"
asks Kaboodle.

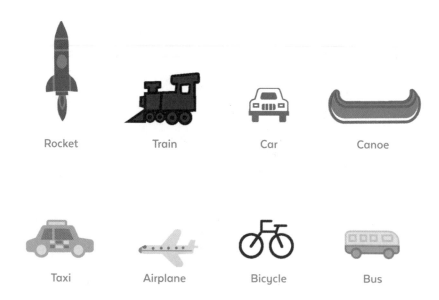

Rocket   Train   Car   Canoe

Taxi   Airplane   Bicycle   Bus

Did you find all the things Kit and

 Airplane

 Bag of Popcorn

 Ball of Yarn

 Balloon

 Canoe

 Car

 Check

 Churro

 Credit Card

 Dollar Bill

 Fan

 Flag

 Hair Dryer

 Horn

 Hot Dog

 Ice-Cream Cone

 Pickle

 Pinwheel

 Playing Cards

 Pompom

 Saltshaker

 Seashell

 Taco

 Taxi

Kaboodle packed for their trip?

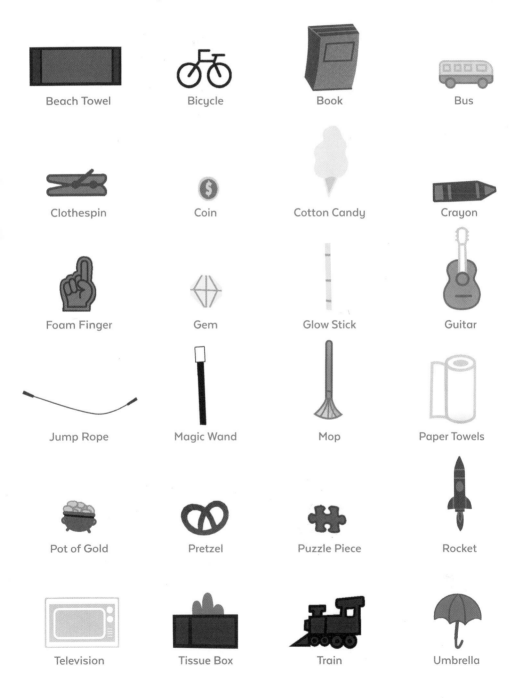

Beach Towel	Bicycle	Book	Bus
Clothespin	Coin	Cotton Candy	Crayon
Foam Finger	Gem	Glow Stick	Guitar
Jump Rope	Magic Wand	Mop	Paper Towels
Pot of Gold	Pretzel	Puzzle Piece	Rocket
Television	Tissue Box	Train	Umbrella

For information about permission to reprint selections from this book,
please contact permissions@highlights.com.

Published by Highlights Press
815 Church Street
Honesdale, Pennsylvania 18431
ISBN (paperback): 978-1-64472-131-5
ISBN (hardcover): 978-1-64472-132-2
ISBN (ebook): 978-1-64472-240-4

Library of Congress Control Number: 2020949605
Manufactured in Melrose Park, IL, USA
Mfg. 03/2021

First edition
Visit our website at Highlights.com.
10 9 8 7 6 5 4 3 2 1

This book has been officially leveled with both the F&P Text Level
Gradient™ Leveling System and the Lexile® Text Measure.

For assistance in the preparation of this book, the editors would like
to thank Vanessa Maldonado, MSEd, MS Literacy Ed. K–12, Reading/LA
Consultant Cert., K–5 Literacy Instructional Coach; and Gina Shaw.